To Phillip M.J.

To Gabriel and Clara A.W.

First North American Edition
Published 1998 by Tommy Nelson™,
a division of Thomas Nelson, Inc.,
Nashville, Tennessee.
ISBN 0-8499-5821-0

A catalog record for this book is available
from the British Library

98 99 00 01 02 Book Print 9 8 7 6 5 4 3 2 1

Printed and bound in Spain

The Good Man of Assisi

Mary Joslin

Illustrations by Alison Wisenfeld

Tommy
NELSON

Thomas Nelson, Inc.
Nashville

Long ago, in the
busy little town of Assisi,
a wealthy merchant
and his wife
had a baby boy.
They wanted
to give
their little son
all the good things
their money could buy.

The boy was called Francis.

He liked poems

and songs

and parties.

He grew up rich.

He grew up strong.

Francis longed to be a knight.
He wanted to show he was strong,
to win great battles
for a powerful lord.

The first time he went to war,
he was taken prisoner.
His friends had to pay
to free him.

The second time he set out,
he had a dream.
He was told to go home
and learn to serve
a different lord,
the Lord God.

But back home in Assisi,
Francis wondered just what to do.
His friends said,
"You know what makes a good party.
You can be lord of our parties."

And so he was.
Francis liked to give
to others and he spent
lots of money
on food and drink.

When everyone was eating and drinking and singing noisy songs, Francis remembered God.

He remembered Jesus, born to show God's goodness to the world.

Francis remembered
words of Jesus
he had read in the Bible:
"Sell what you have
and give the money to
poor people.
And come, follow me."
Francis took off his fine clothes
and gave them to the poor.

Jesus said,
"Anyone who wants to
follow me must give up
everything else."
Francis left his home
to go about the world
telling people of Jesus.

Jesus loved those
who were not strong.
He healed the sick.
So Francis helped people
who were ill and was
a friend to those
who were weak.

Above all, Jesus said,
"Love one another
as I have loved you."

Some people
think only of themselves.
Francis helped others.

Some people
find things to
hate about others.
Francis looked for
the good in everyone.

Some people get angry
and shout.
Francis spoke gently
and tried to bring peace.

Some people are sad.
Some have no one who loves
them. Some have bad things
happen to them.

Francis was a friend to them.
He showed them
that God loved them.
And he gave them hope.

More and more people
came to see Francis
and hear what
he had to say.

Many people
changed their lives
to live more
like Jesus.

Some decided to
live like Francis.
They were
known as friars.

Others stayed at home
living simply,
loving greatly,
and making their world
more gentle
and lovely.

Francis believed
everything
was made by God
and was very, very good.

So he admired
the little things.
He loved the wriggly
worms and would stop
to lift them from harm.

He admired the great
and wonderful things
of the world.
He loved the golden sun
of daytime and the
moon and stars
in the night sky.

 He wanted the flowers
to sing to God their Maker.

He wanted all
the lovely things
of earth and fire,
air and water
to love their Maker...

to show their love
by doing the things
for which God
had created them.

All things he called
brother or sister,
and living things loved him
and followed him.

Francis talked to
the birds about
God their Maker.

He told them always to
thank God who gave
them clear air to fly in
and food to eat.

Then Francis said a prayer for them,
and let them fly away,
singing God's praises.

In the same way, Francis
told all birds, animals
and reptiles to praise God
and to love God.

 And Francis wanted all people
to praise God, and to remember
that God, who is rich beyond all
dreaming, had come to earth
as a poor baby—the baby Jesus.

One December,
Francis asked a good man
he knew to prepare a stable
like the one in Bethlehem
so long before,
where Jesus had been
cradled in a manger.

Men and women saw the stable
and remembered Jesus.

In time, Francis
grew weak and ill.
He remembered that God,
who is strong beyond
all imagining, had come to earth as Jesus
and become weak.

Angry people had put Jesus to death
on a cross of wood.

Francis wanted to follow Jesus
in every way and, by a miracle,
he was given the same wounds
that Jesus had on his hands,
his feet and his side.

Francis died poor. He died weak.
But he died gladly. He trusted Jesus' promise
that death would take him close to God—
safe forever.

Lord, make me a channel of your peace.

Where there is hatred, let me sow love,

Where there is injury, pardon,

Where there is doubt, faith,

Where there is despair, hope,

Where there is darkness, light,

Where there is sadness, joy.

O Divine Master, grant that I may not

so much seek to be consoled as to console,

not so much to be understood as to understand,

not so much to be loved as to love;

for it is in giving that we receive,

it is in pardoning that we are pardoned,

it is in dying that we awake to eternal life.

A prayer for those who want to follow Jesus as Francis did